MEM FOX

Tough Boris

Illustrated by

KATHRYN BROWN

Harcourt, Inc.

Orlando Austin New York San Diego Toronto London

With special thanks to Allyn Johnston, Janet Green,

Joe, Paul, BZ, and Eric

—K. B.

Text copyright © 1994 by Mem Fox
Illustrations copyright © 1994 by Kathryn Brown

www.HarcourtBooks.com

Library of Congress Cataloging-in-Publication Data
Fox, Mem, 1946–
Tough Boris/Mem Fox: illustrated by Kathryn Brown. —1st ed.
p. cm.
Summary: Boris von der Borch is a tough pirate,
but he cries when his parrot dies.
ISBN 0-15-289612-0
[1. Pirates — Fiction.]   I. Brown, Kathryn, 1955– ill.
II. Title.
PZ7.F8373To   1994
[E]—dc20   92-8015

L N P R S Q O M K

The illustrations in this book were done in watercolors on Waterford paper.
The display and text type were set in Cochin by Harcourt, Inc.
Photocomposition Center, San Diego, California.
Color separations by Bright Arts, Ltd., Singapore
Printed and bound by Tien Wah Press, Singapore
Production supervision by Warren Wallerstein and Kent MacElwee
Designed by Camilla Filancia

Printed in Singapore

For Alexia and Helen
and, of course,
Paul von der Borch
—M. F.

For Parker, Sawyer, Will,
Levi, and Amos
—K. B.

Once upon a time, there lived a
pirate named Boris von der Borch.

He was tough.

All pirates are tough.

He was massive.
All pirates are massive.

He was scruffy.

All pirates are scruffy.

He was greedy.

All pirates are greedy.

He was fearless.

All pirates
are fearless.

He was scary.

All pirates are scary.

But when his parrot died,

he cried and cried.

All pirates cry.

And so do I.